Eva
the Enchanted Ball
Fairy

To Leila-Mai Burge with lots of love

Special thanks to
Sue Mongredien

ORCHARD BOOKS
338 Euston Road, London NW1 3BH
Orchard Books Australia
Level 17/207 Kent Street, Sydney, NSW 2000
A Paperback Original

First published in 2011 by Orchard Books

HiT entertainment

A CIP catalogue record for this book is available
from the British Library.

ISBN 978 1 40831 299 5

7 9 10 8

Printed in Great Britain

The paper and board used in this paperback are natural recyclable
products made from wood grown in sustainable forests. The
manufacturing processes conform to the environmental regulations
of the country of origin.

Orchard Books is a division of Hachette Children's Books,
an Hachette UK company

www.hachette.co.uk

Eva
the Enchanted Ball
Fairy

by Daisy Meadows

ORCHARD

www.rainbowmagic.co.uk

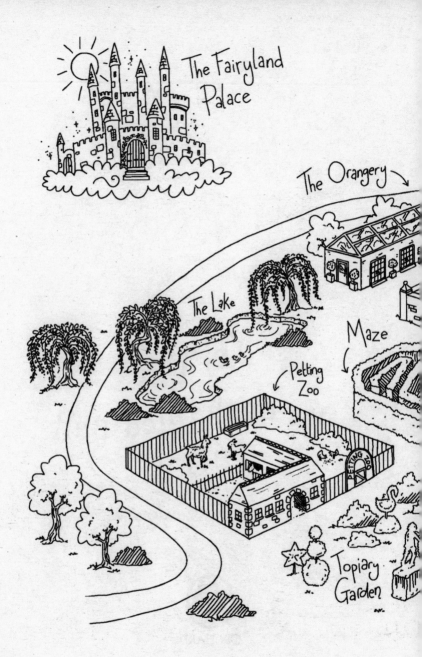

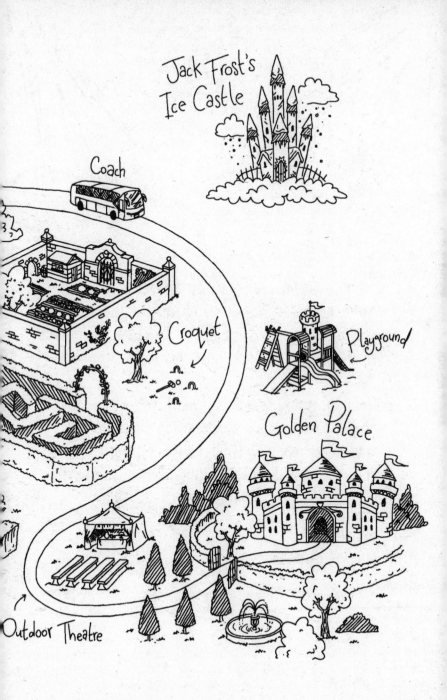

The fairies are planning a magical ball,
With guests of honour and fun for them all.
They're expecting a night full of laughter and cheer
But they'll get a shock when my goblins appear!

Adventures and treats will be things of the past,
And I'll beat those troublesome fairies at last.
My iciest magic will blast through the room
And the world will be plunged into grimness
and gloom!

Contents

A Dancing Disaster

"One-two-three, one-two-three, one-two-three," murmured Rachel Walker under her breath, trying to concentrate on what her feet were doing. She and her best friend, Kirsty Tate, were staying at Golden Palace for Kids' Week, an activity holiday. Today they were in the ballroom, enjoying a dancing lesson.

The ballroom was very grand, with huge glittering chandeliers hanging from the ceiling, and dark-red velvety wallpaper.

It was the last full day of the holiday and Kirsty and Rachel had had lots of fun. They'd been on a treasure hunt, taken part in a sports day and a pageant, enjoyed a tea party in the palace gardens, and much more. It had been so exciting to stay in a real palace too, with a drawbridge, and moat, and gold-topped towers. Best of all, the girls had also found themselves on another wonderful fairy adventure, this time with the Princess Fairies!

A Grand Ball was taking place that evening, and everyone was planning on dressing up in their nicest clothes. Louis and Caroline, the staff members who had looked after the children all week, were teaching them the waltz, but nobody was finding it very easy.

"Whoops," said one boy, accidentally treading on his partner's toes.

"Sorry," said a girl as she swung around too energetically and bumped into the person behind her.

"Ow," said Kirsty, as she stumbled, knocking against one of the tables at the far end of the room. The table had been decorated with flower arrangements and elegant glass vases filled

with colourful sweets, ready for the ball that evening. One of the vases toppled over and Kirsty only just caught it before it hit the floor.

"Oh dear," sighed Louis, swapping a glance with Caroline. "This isn't going as well as I'd hoped."

Kirsty and Rachel looked at one another too. They had a good idea why everyone was finding it hard to learn the waltz — and it was all because of Jack Frost!

At the start of the week, the girls had been magically whisked to Fairyland where a special ball was being held in honour of the seven Princess Fairies. But mean Jack Frost had turned up uninvited with his goblins and had stolen the Princess Fairies' magic tiaras and taken them to the human world.

The Princess Fairies usually used their magic to look after all sorts of things — dressing-up, playtime, adventures and happy occasions — but without their tiaras, their magic wasn't working and fun occasions were turning into disasters!

Luckily, Queen Titania had been able to cast a spell to ensure that the seven tiaras ended up in Golden Palace, and ever since then, Kirsty and Rachel had been tracking them down. So far, they'd found six of the stolen tiaras but there was still one missing, which belonged to Princess Eva the Enchanted Ball Fairy.

"Unless we find Princess Eva's tiara, tonight's ball is going to be a disaster," Rachel whispered to Kirsty. "We've got to keep a lookout for it."

Kirsty nodded, just as Caroline turned off the music and clapped her hands for silence. "I'm afraid we've run out of time for our dance class," she said.

"Don't worry if you're not sure about
the steps yet – we'll still have plenty of
fun later on at the ball."

All the children left the ballroom and
started making their way upstairs to get
changed for the
ball. Kirsty
and Rachel
clattered up
the grand
main
staircase
and along
to the
tower
where
they were
sharing a
bedroom.

"I'm going to wear the party dress that Phoebe the Fashion Fairy made me," Kirsty said as they walked along.

"Me too!" Rachel said, smiling

They'd helped Phoebe and her friends the Party Fairies during another holiday, and Phoebe had rewarded the girls with a beautiful new dress each. Even though both girls had grown taller since then, their dresses still fitted perfectly, as if there was magic sewn into the seams.

But up in their bedroom, Rachel pulled open the wardrobe doors and the girls had a horrible surprise. Kirsty's pink dress had a dark stain down the front which hadn't been there before, and Rachel's lilac dress now had a large rip in one of the sleeves.

"Oh no," Kirsty exclaimed. "Our dresses look more like Cinderella's rags than beautiful ballgowns. What are we going to do?"

Flight to Fairyland

Just then, the girls heard a rustling sound and out of the wardrobe flew a tiny, blonde fairy. She was wearing a glittery pink ballgown that billowed elegantly around her, and lilac shoes that seemed to be set with tiny gems. The girls smiled as they recognised Princess Eva the Enchanted Ball Fairy.

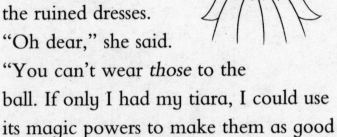

"Hello,"
Princess Eva
said, smiling –
then her face
fell as she saw
the ruined dresses.
"Oh dear," she said.
"You can't wear *those* to the
ball. If only I had my tiara, I could use
its magic powers to make them as good
as new for you."

"We can wear something else," Kirsty
said, turning away from the ruined
dresses. "But more importantly, we can
help you look for your tiara."

"Definitely," Rachel agreed. "We
know that Jack Frost and his goblins are
hiding out in one of the towers. Why
don't we search around there?"

"Thank you," Princess Eva replied.
"First, let me turn you into fairies.
We can fly up there together then."
She waved her wand and a stream of
rainbow-coloured sparkles billowed out
from it, swirling all around the girls. In
the next moment, they felt themselves
shrinking smaller and smaller until they
were the same size as Eva – and had
their own gauzy fairy
wings, too!

Kirsty beamed
as she fluttered
her wings
and swooped
around the
room. Being
a fairy was the
best thing ever!

"Let's go," Eva said, and led them out of the room and along to the old tower which Jack Frost had made his hideout. Then they flew up the spiral staircase together, high above the crumbling stone steps. As they neared the top of the tower, the air grew much colder and icicles appeared on the walls.

"Hmmm," Eva said, a worried expression on her face. "It looks like Jack Frost is up to something. I think it must be his icy magic which has caused the temperature to drop so low. Come on, let's investigate."

At the top of the staircase, there was a large wooden door which was slightly ajar. The three fairies peeped around it to see Jack Frost and his goblins inside, with whizzing swirls of icy blue magic crackling all around them. Jack Frost was wearing Eva's tiara as he addressed the goblins. "Good news!" he cackled. "The spell cast by Queen Titania, which kept all the Princess Fairies' tiaras at Golden Palace, is wearing off.

So we can take this tiara to my Ice Castle," he went on gloatingly, "and we'll have the most amazing ball ever — way better than a stupid fairy ball."

With that, he clapped his hands, and the icy blue magic surged at him and the goblins with a rushing sound. There was a sudden shower of ice chips…and then he and the goblins vanished.

"We'll have to go after them," Rachel said. "We've got to get that tiara back!"

"Yes," Eva said. "And there's no time to delay. To Fairyland!" She waved her wand and more of the rainbow-coloured sparkles burst all around the fairies, whirling them out of the tower and away.

When the magic whirlwind slowed and lowered the three fairies to the ground once more, Kirsty, Rachel and Eva found themselves outside Jack Frost's Ice Castle in Fairyland. It was a forbidding place, extremely cold and made of glittering blue ice, but as the girls peered through the windows into the great hall, they realised that today everything seemed jollier.

Jack Frost was busy preparing for his ball. He raised his hand, firing an icy bolt of magic – and in the next instant, blue and green decorations appeared around the room. *Zap!* There went another icy bolt, making silver trays appear on a table, piled high with ice lollies and bowls of ice cream.

Zap! Ballroom music started playing. With a final wave of his hand, Jack Frost zapped an outfit for himself – an ice-blue robe and bow tie. He was still wearing Eva's magic tiara, Rachel noticed.

As the fairies watched, the goblins began pouring into the room, all wearing their party clothes.

"Let the Ice Castle Ball begin!" Jack Frost declared grandly, and the goblins cheered.

But before long, things started to go wrong. Kirsty put her hands over her ears as the music changed to horrible banging sounds. The ice cream and ice lollies started melting stickily on the silver trays, the decorations blew off the walls in a sudden draught, and the goblins' clothes looked tatty and torn. Jack Frost tried to get everyone dancing to the awful music but the goblins didn't want to, and began pushing each other around and jumping on the tables instead.

Eva winced as the music banged and crashed even more loudly. "Jack Frost might think he can have the perfect ball because he's got my tiara, but he's wrong," she said. "Unless I have the tiara, no one — not even Jack Frost — can have a successful ball."

"Oh dear," Rachel said. "Look at him now. He's furious!"

Jack Frost stamped his foot in rage. "This is not good enough," he fumed. "I wanted a proper ball — with elegant outfits, beautiful decorations, lovely music and graceful dancing.

Nothing has gone right. This stupid fairy tiara is rubbish!"

"I wonder…" said Rachel thoughtfully to herself. "Yes, that might work…"

"What might work?" Kirsty asked.

Rachel smiled, her eyes shining. "I've had an idea," she said. "If Jack Frost wants the perfect ball – then we'll give him one!"

Flying Ice Cream

Rachel explained her plan. "Eva, if you could use some magic to disguise me as a party organiser, I might be able to get into the Ice Castle pretending I'm there to help Jack Frost," she said. "Hopefully once I'm inside I can find a way to sneak the tiara off his head and get it back to you."

Eva looked uncertain. "I like the party organiser idea," she said, "but it might be risky to try to get my tiara. We've already seen what a vile mood Jack Frost is in – he could turn really nasty."

"Maybe we could fly in as well," Kirsty suggested. "And then while Rachel is helping Jack Frost we might be able to grab the tiara without him noticing us."

"Good thinking," Eva said, and waved her wand. "One party organiser coming up!"

Rainbow sparkles poured from her wand and tumbled about Rachel. When they cleared away, Rachel was dressed in bright party clothes and a sparkly wig, carrying bunches of balloons and a bag of party streamers.

Kirsty grinned. "Good luck," she said.

"You too," Rachel said. "Let's do it!"

Kirsty and Eva fluttered through an open window while Rachel knocked on the door of the castle. When Jack Frost opened it with a suspicious glare, she smiled politely and said, "Hello, I'm from Perfect Party Services. I gather your ball isn't going quite to plan. May I be of assistance?"

The frown vanished from Jack Frost's face and a look of relief appeared in its place. "Yes, please," he said, throwing the door wide so that Rachel could step in. "You're just what I need.

Come in, come in."

Kirsty and Eva fluttered to a dark
corner of the room and hovered in the
shadows, watching as Rachel showed
Jack Frost how to blow up balloons.
"Splendid," she said cheerfully, tying
neat knots in the balloon ends. "And
now for some

streamers –
I've got some
lovely sparkly
ones here,"
she said,
pulling them
out of her
bag. "These
will make
the room look
fantastic."

While Jack Frost was admiring the
streamers and draping them over the
grey candleholders on the walls, Kirsty
and Eva seized the chance to fly nearer
to him. They swooped down to the table
laden with melting ice creams and hid
behind it, waiting for the right moment
to flutter out and grab the tiara.

The goblins, meanwhile, were getting
bored. One of them
threw a scoop
of ice cream
at another,
chuckling
as it
splattered
on the
second
goblin's head.

"Hey!" the second goblin spluttered.
"Two can play at that game!" And
he hurled a lump of ice cream back. It
wasn't long before all the goblins were
throwing ice cream around
the room, making
a terrible
mess.

Jack
Frost
was busy
arranging
his new
streamers
and ignored
them. Then, as he
walked nearer to the food table to pin up
some of the balloons, Kirsty and Rachel
exchanged meaningful glances.

"Now!" Eva whispered, and she and Kirsty both zoomed out of their hiding place and up towards the tiara on Jack Frost's head. But unfortunately for the fairies, as they were fluttering through the air, Kirsty was hit by the flying ice cream and let out a squeak of shock.

"Hey," called a goblin. "I just saw a fairy. Two fairies!"

Kirsty and Eva veered away in fright

as the goblins began chasing them around the room. One goblin, who wasn't looking where he was going, crashed into Jack Frost, sending him skidding through an ice-cream puddle along the floor. "Behave yourselves!" Jack Frost roared at the goblins. "You're ruining this ball!"

Rachel's eyes widened as she caught sight of Kirsty and Eva being pursued. She lifted a corner of the tablecloth, and gestured to the panicky fairies to fly down and hide there.

"But we've seen some fairies," one of the goblins was protesting to Jack Frost. "We're only trying to get rid of them for you."

"Fairies?" thundered Jack Frost, and Rachel trembled at the fury in his voice.

"I…I think they went that way," she said quickly, pointing out of the window, and hoping desperately that he would believe her.

Jack Frost ran outside immediately in search of the fairies, with the goblins following. Eva and Kirsty flew out from their hiding place, their hearts pounding. "That didn't work too well," Rachel said.

Eva waved her wand at Rachel, turning her back into a fairy. "We need to think of a new plan," she said, but then broke off hurriedly as they heard the sound of footsteps returning.

"Jack Frost's coming back," she hissed. "Quick – hide!"

Trapped in Chains

The fairies dived behind the ice-cream bowls once more as the door was flung open with a crash, and Jack Frost stomped back inside. He looked around and gave an enormous sigh. "Even the party planner has had enough of my ball," he said glumly. He sat on his throne looking thoroughly fed up as he stared at the mess the goblins had made.

Kirsty and Rachel were surprised to find that they actually felt sorry for Jack Frost. They'd been looking forward to the ball at Golden Palace, so they could imagine how disappointed he must feel, now that his own ball had gone wrong. Even his smart cape had got covered in ice cream when he'd fallen over.

"I wonder if… " Kirsty began in a low voice, then shook her head. "No," she said in the next breath. "I don't think it would work."

"What?" Eva whispered.

"Well, I was just wondering if there was any chance we could hold another Fairyland Ball and invite Jack Frost to come this time," Kirsty said. "But I know he doesn't deserve to go, after everything he's done."

Eva gazed at Jack Frost, her head on one side. "I don't know if we can trust him to behave," she said doubtfully after a moment. "He might just try to spoil everything again."

"Maybe the thought of dancing, delicious food and lots of fun will persuade him to be nice," Rachel suggested. "He'd have to give up the tiara first, of course."

"Absolutely," Eva agreed. "And apologise, too. Let's see what he thinks." The three fairies flew out from their hiding place and hovered in front of Jack Frost, who was still moping on the throne.

"Hi there," Kirsty began timidly. "We were just wondering if you might…"

But before she could get any further, Jack Frost had clutched the tiara to his head with a look of panic. "You're not getting *this* back," he hissed, and fired three bursts of icy magic at the fairies. *Zap! Zap! Zap!*

One of the ice-bolts hit a chain of streamers which fell down from the ceiling, landing on the fairies and sending them plummeting to the ground. They lay on the cold stone floor, struggling to get out of the paper chains while Jack Frost approached, icy magic crackling around his fingertips.

Eva wrestled her wand free and
pointed it quickly at Jack Frost,
muttering a magic spell. Glittery sparkles
began to whirl
around his
head so
fast that
Jack Frost
couldn't
see the
fairies.

"What I
was trying
to tell you,"
Kirsty called up
while he was busy zapping the sparkles
away with ice-bolts, "was that we want
to invite you to a Fairyland Ball."

"I'll clean up your new outfit so you

can show it off," Eva went on, "and there will be dancing, and the Fairyland Orchestra playing beautiful music…"

"There will be lovely food, too," Rachel said, as melted ice cream dripped loudly off the tables onto the floor.

Jack Frost looked excited for a moment, but then his expression became suspicious. "Sounds too good to be true," he muttered darkly. "What's the catch?"

"All you have to do," Kirsty told him, "is apologise to Eva, and hand back her tiara. What do you think?"

An Extra Guest

There were a tense few moments while the fairy friends waited for Jack Frost's response. Kirsty and Rachel were expecting him to sneer at their offer, and were braced for more bolts of icy magic to come their way. To their surprise, though, he just nodded abruptly.

"Sorry," he muttered through gritted teeth. He scooped the paper chains off the fairies, then held the tiara out towards Eva. "All right, you can have it back, I suppose," he said, peevishly.

Eva beamed as she shook out her wings and fluttered up into the air. Kirsty and Rachel flew up too, glad to be free once more and able to fly. Eva gave her

wand a deft flick and the tiara shrank down to fairy size and then whizzed through the air, landing neatly on Eva's head.

She put a hand up to touch it and looked happier than Kirsty and Rachel had ever seen her. "Thank you," she said, dropping a polite curtsey to Jack Frost. "That was the right thing to do. Now  I have my Enchanted Ball magic once more, and I can use it to make a night we'll all remember! Let me see…I'll do outfits first."

She waved her wand in Jack Frost's
direction and the ice-cream stains
vanished from his smart cape,
much to his delight.
Then she
waved her
wand at
Kirsty and
Rachel,
and their
clothes
transformed
into the
most beautiful
ballgowns they'd ever
seen. Rachel was now wearing
a lilac gown with gathered folds of silk,
and Kirsty wore a pink gown with layers
of yellow tulle. Both girls had matching

tiaras woven with rosebuds and sparkling silver jewels.

"You look just like a princess," Kirsty marvelled, beaming at Rachel. "So do you!" Rachel replied happily. Eva smiled proudly at their words. "Now to make our way to the Fairyland Palace," she said. "Let's go outside and I'll rustle up the perfect transport to take us there."

Outside, the goblins had given up
fairy-hunting and were hurling snowballs
at each other. With another wave of her
wand, Eva conjured up a horse-drawn
glass carriage, just like the one in which
the Princess Fairies had first arrived
at the palace, at the start of the girls'
adventure. The four white horses looked
very grand in their purple and gold
harnesses with matching feathery plumes
on their heads.

"Cool!" marvelled one of the goblins. "Is that for us?"

"There's not room for you, I'm afraid," Eva replied, "but you can follow behind us on these." She waved her wand again, and some magnificent golden toboggans appeared on the snow. The goblins whooped with excitement and ran over to them. One goblin even managed to remember a "Thank you!".

Kirsty, Rachel, Eva and Jack Frost
climbed into the glass carriage, and
the four horses began trotting carefully
through the snow.

"You're like a Fairy Godmother, Eva,"
Rachel said, unable
to stop smiling.
"This is all so
wonderful."

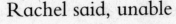

"It might
be all right, I
suppose," Jack
Frost agreed,
fingering his bow
tie. "With someone
as handsome as me there!"

It didn't take the horses long to arrive
at the palace, and as the carriage came
to a stop, the palace doors burst open.

Down the
marble steps
hurried King
Oberon,
Queen
Titania and
the six other
Princess
Fairies, all
overjoyed
to see the
safe return
of Kirsty,
Rachel and Eva.

The three friends climbed out and
said hello, but Jack Frost stayed in the
carriage, looking rather awkward. He
wasn't sure that he'd be welcomed by
the other fairies.

"I have my tiara back, and I'd like to throw a celebratory ball for everyone," Eva declared. "And the guests of honour will be Kirsty and Rachel, who have helped us so bravely and kindly."

"Hurrah!" the other fairies cheered.

Kirsty felt her cheeks turn red. "It was

fun," she said. "Thanks for asking us."

"We've invited an extra guest to the ball," Rachel said. "Someone who's had a change of heart recently. Jack Frost!"

A gasp went up around the fairies, as Jack Frost clambered out of the carriage and stood before them. The smiles had vanished from everyone's faces.

"Are you sure he can be trusted?" King Oberon asked suspiciously, and Kirsty and Rachel held their breath. Was their plan of inviting Jack Frost about to go horribly wrong?

Having a Ball

Jack Frost glared at the king and queen. Then he swallowed hard.

"I'm sorry," he muttered. "I promise I will be on my best behaviour for the ball. So will the goblins."

The king and queen exchanged a glance, and Queen Titania gave a little nod. "In that case, you're welcome here," she said.

Princess Eva raised her wand once more. "Let the ball begin!" she declared.

It wasn't long before the ball was in full swing. The Fairyland Orchestra played wonderful music, everyone wore their best clothes and danced all evening. Some of the Dance Fairies helped Kirsty and Rachel practise their ballroom dancing steps until they both felt confident about their footwork.

True to their promise, Jack Frost
and the goblins behaved themselves
and showed fairly good table manners
when the banquet was served, with
only a small food fight while the plates
were being cleared away. And Princess
Eva was the perfect hostess, using her
Enchanted Ball magic to make sure that
everyone had a fantastic time.

Then, as the clock struck midnight, the music stopped, and the king, the queen and the Princess Fairies all approached Kirsty and Rachel.

"It's time for you to return to your own world," Queen Titania said, taking Kirsty and Rachel by the hands. "Thank you once again – and we hope to see you soon."

"And enjoy the ball at Golden Palace," Eva added with a smile. "I have a feeling it's going to be every bit as enchanting as this one."

Rachel and Kirsty
just managed to say
goodbye to all
their fairy friends
before they
were spun up
in a magical
sparkly
whirlwind
which took
them back
to Golden
Palace.
They found
themselves in
their bedrooms
again, still wearing the beautiful
ballgowns and tiaras Eva had
given them.

"Look at our party dresses – they're perfect now," Rachel said, pulling hers out of the wardrobe. "Eva must have used her magic to make them as good as new again."

"I'm still going to keep my ballgown on, aren't you?" Kirsty said, twirling happily in front of the mirror.

"Definitely," Rachel replied. "Come on, let's go downstairs. The Grand Ball should be starting any minute." She giggled. "I feel every bit as princessy as the Princess Fairies themselves, going to our second ball of the evening," she said. "Especially dressed like this!"

Kirsty and Rachel made their way down to the ballroom where lots of people were already dancing. Kirsty was sure she spotted some extra fairy lights around the room which hadn't been there before – and the ceiling seemed to be decorated with tiny twinkling stars too! Were they thanks to Eva's magic? she wondered with a smile.

The music sounded great and everyone was enjoying themselves as they danced. Nobody was treading on each other's toes or tripping over now, and the girls knew it was because Princess Eva had her magic tiara back. Hurrah for fairy magic!

"We've had such fun here," Kirsty said, waving to some of the other children who were wearing dresses almost as lovely as hers. "I'm going to be sad to leave Golden Palace tomorrow."

"Me too," Rachel said, gazing around at Caroline and Louis, Mrs King the palace cook and Jean the animal keeper, who were all dressed in their finery and dancing happily. "But I'm sure this won't be the last of our fairy adventures, Kirsty." She grinned. "Now…may I have this dance?"

Laughing, Kirsty took Rachel's hands. "You may," she replied in her best princess voice. And the two girls spun on to the dancefloor together.

Now it's time for Kirsty and Rachel to help...

Natalie the Christmas Stocking Fairy

Read on for a sneak peek...

"I love making mince pies," said Rachel Walker, sieving flour and salt into a heavy mixing bowl.

"Me too," said her best friend Kirsty Tate, opening the jar of mincemeat and taking a deep sniff. "It's such a spicy, Christmassy smell!"

She put the lid back on the jar and the girls smiled happily at each other. It was the day before Christmas Eve, and they were staying in a cosy holiday cottage in the country with their families.

"Woof!" said Rachel's dog.

"You're looking forward to Christmas

too, aren't you, Buttons?" said Kirsty, leaning down to stroke his shaggy head.

"What does the recipe say next?" asked Rachel.

Kirsty stood up and looked at the recipe book that was propped on the kitchen counter.

"Rub the butter in with your fingers until the mixture looks like fine crumbs," she read out.

Rachel opened the fridge and frowned.

"Kirsty, have you already taken the butter out of the fridge?"

"No," said Kirsty in surprise.

"That's funny," said Rachel. "I was sure we had some."

"Maybe we put it somewhere else," Kirsty suggested. "Let's look around."

They hunted high and low, but the

butter was nowhere to be found. It was very strange.

"We'll just have to go to the shops again," said Rachel.

"But we're miles from anywhere," Kirsty said with a groan. "And it's nearly closing time."

Just then, Mr Tate walked into the kitchen looking puzzled...

Read **Natalie the Christmas Stocking Fairy** to find out what adventures are in store for Kirsty and Rachel!

Meet the Princess Fairies

Honor
the Happy Days
Fairy

Demi
the Dressing-Up
Fairy

Anya
the Cuddly Creatures
Fairy

Elisa
the Adventure
Fairy

Lizzie
the Sweet Treats
Fairy

Maddie
the Playtime
Fairy

Eva
the Enchanted Ball
Fairy

Jack Frost has stolen the Princess Fairies' special tiaras.
Kirsty and Rachel must get them back, or all the
magic in the world will fade away!

www.rainbowmagicbooks.co.uk

Meet the fairies, play games
and get sneak peeks at
the latest books!

www.rainbowmagicbooks.co.uk

There's fairy fun for everyone on
our wonderful website.
You'll find great activities, competitions, stories and
fairy profiles, and also a special newsletter.

Get 30% off all Rainbow Magic books at

www.rainbowmagicbooks.co.uk

Enter the code RAINBOW at the checkout.
Offer ends 31 December 2013.

Offer valid in United Kingdom and Republic of Ireland only.